LONE WOLF and CUB

by
KAZUO KOIKE
and
GOSEKI KOJIMA

LYNN VARLEY

第11巻　　小島剛夕　小池一夫

FIRST PUBLISHING

Kazuo Koike
STORY

Goseki Kojima
ART

Frank Miller
COVER ILLUSTRATION & INTRODUCTION

David Lewis and Alex Wald
ENGLISH ADAPTATION

Willie Schubert
LETTERING

Paul Guinan
PRODUCTION

Rick Oliver
EDITOR

Rick Obadiah
PUBLISHER

Alex Wald
ART DIRECTOR

Kathy Kotsivas
OPERATIONS DIRECTOR

Rick Taylor
PRODUCTION MANAGER

Kurt Goldzung
SALES DIRECTOR

Published monthly in the United States of America by First Comics, Inc., 435 N. LaSalle, Chicago Il 60610, and Studio Ship, Inc. under exclusive license by Global Communications Corporation, Musashiya Building, 4th Floor, 27-10, Aobadai 1-Chome, Meguro-Ku, Tokyo, 153 Japan, owner of world wide publishing rights to the property Lone Wolf and Cub.

First printing, March 1988.

or a long time, the term "comic book" has, in America, been for many a movie or literary critic an easy way to damn a piece of work as cheap, worthless entertainment. It's been hard to argue with them, even for us who love comics; in America, artists and publishers have done very little to prove that comics are anything more.

And, after all, an artform is only as good as its practitioners.

Thing is, there have been some extraordinary talents at work in American comics, though rarely have they been properly paid or even credited for what they've given us. Were everything in the world right and just, and had American comics publishers of past decades had the least respect for what they published and for the artists who wrote and drew it, the names of Jack Kirby, Will Eisner, Carl Barks, and Harvey Kurtzman would be as familiar as those of George Lucas, Steven Spielberg, and Walt Disney.

Just about all of the really terrific work in American comics has been buried in popular history and ignored by popular historians — though all the while film makers and television producers alike have strip-mined the field. The stories, ideas, designs, and concepts of those precious few genuine artists in comics have been lifted whole and translated into box office sensations like *Star Wars* and *Superman*.

It's very different in Japan, where comics have come to be accepted as a worthy story form — and a vastly popular one.

One of the most popular, boasting sales in the many millions and faithful adaptations to television and film, is Kazuo Koike's and Goseki Kojima's *Lone Wolf and Cub*, a nine thousand page epic adventure featuring a rogue samurai warrior and his son, surviving against a beautifully detailed tapestry of decadent Japan.

Each chapter of *Lone Wolf and Cub* sheds light upon another facet of the fatalistic, proud code of honor of the samurai, describing, in terms that are vastly unlike our own, what it is that makes the perfect warrior, even as it examines his ultimate futility and the utter tragedy of war.

This segment is one of the most compelling and poignant. A doomed young boy in a doomed land must prove himself as much a samurai as his father. Fearlessly, he carries on the dark legacy...

Frank Miller
Los Angeles 1988

別れ霜　其之十二　PARTING FROST

Perhaps it had been built by the *peasants* for a moment's *respite* from their labors. It was a small, rotting *tea pavillion*, perched upon a low hill that might once have been the footings of a castle. There the boy waited, watching the rain.

With each rainfall, the approach of spring sent the too-long winter into flight.

But to a small child, it was a rain to freeze the skin... and the heart.

But yet...

To the chill, the hunger, the loneliness...

To all these he was tragically accustomed. A child of fate.

3

So, too, he was accustomed to waiting for his father.

Only...

His father should have returned on the second morning.

But the third morning came. Then the fourth night.

And the fifth morning brought only the rain.

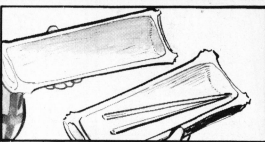

Rather than wait for his father...

Rather than starve and die...

...the boy resolved to find his father himself. He was a boy with a hero's heart.

He was a child who knew that his father lived in the heat of battle.

And if his father never returned, then one of the blood splattered corpses he had so often seen--

--might belong to his father, too. This the child comprehended.

5

Step on a
flower, feel
for the
flower.

It was a
child's spring.

He realized the
futility of asking
strangers about
the father they
had never seen.

He realized he
must **search**,
by his power,
alone.

A tearless...

silent...

child.

9

He knew that
his father, the
assassin's
duty done...

Would always kneel...

before the Buddha.

A child who had witnessed his father...

kill the Buddha.

Why did his father direct his feet to these ancient temples?

Did he come to speak with mother in Yomi, the land of the dead?

Did he come to heal his spirit in the pure, clear air?

The reason was unclear.

Yet he sought his father's shape among the ancient temple shadows.

PAPA!

13

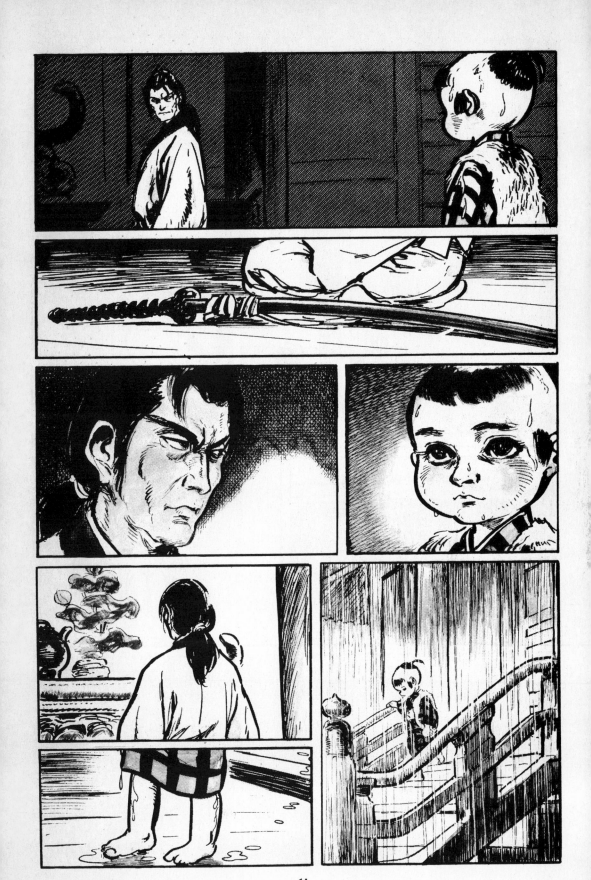

Until finally, at which temple he had lost count, hunger and fatigue overcame him.

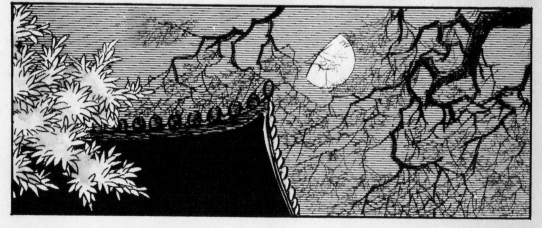

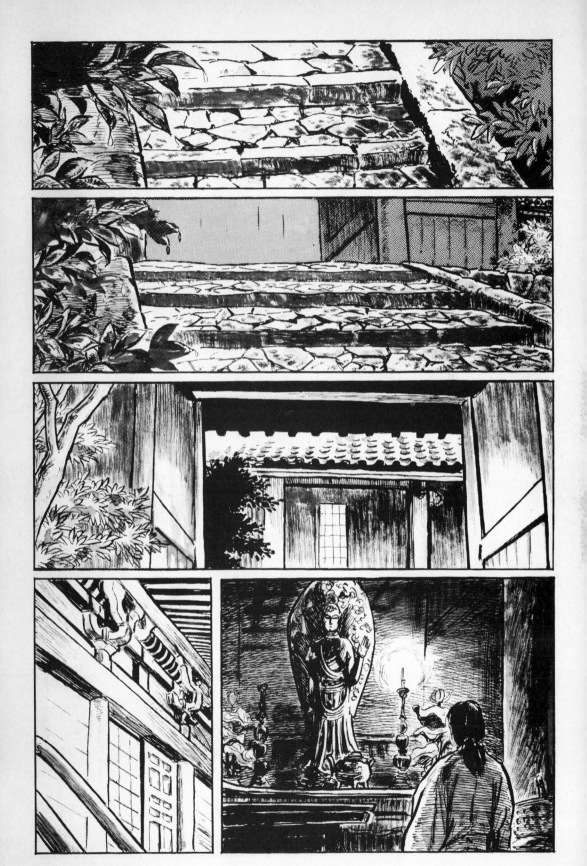

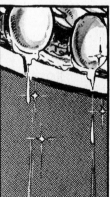

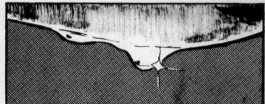

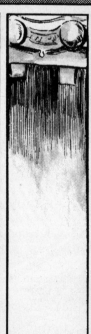

SPLCK

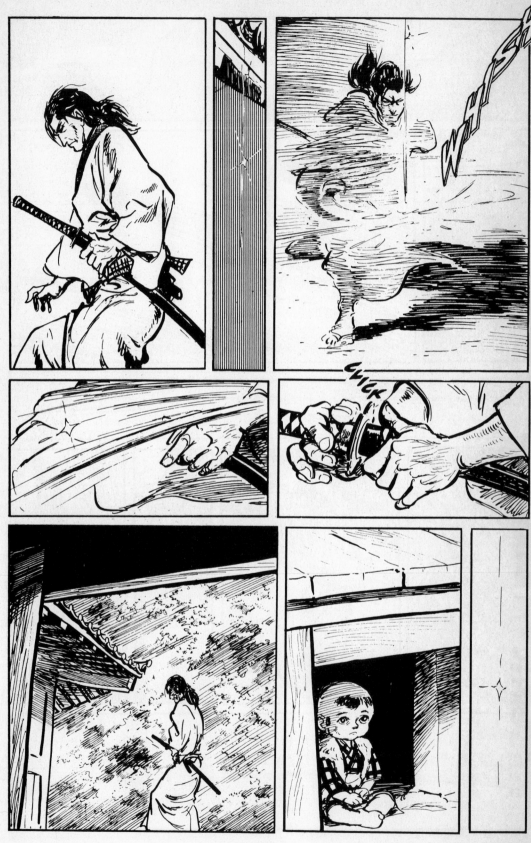

THOSE EYES... LIKE THE SHISHOGAN EYES* OF A MASTER SWORDSMAN...

...PLACING HIMSELF BETWEEN LIFE AND DEATH, ONE WITH THE NOTHINGNESS OF MU.

IMPOSSIBLE! A TINY CHILD? HOW?

I DON'T UNDERSTAND.

ARE MY OWN EYES FAILING ME, TO READ SHISHOGAN IN THAT FACE?

*SHISHOGAN EYES -- THE EYES THAT ONLY ONE WHO HAS STOOD ON THE KILLING FIELDS, WHO HAS LIVED THROUGH COUNTLESS SLAUGHTERS, SHOULD HAVE.

NO ONE COULD *BLAME* HIM FOR TAKING IT.

TRADING HIS OWN CLOTHES FOR FOOD. THERE'S MORE *NOBILITY* IN THAT SINGLE GESTURE THAN MOST MEN HAVE. *SHISHOGAN* OR NOT, HE'S NO NORMAL CHILD.

27

I CAN'T JUST STAND BY!

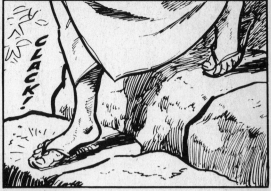

CLACK!

IT'S THE PERFECT CHANCE TO *TEST* THOSE SHISHOGAN EYES!

IF THOSE EYES TRULY KNOW NO *FEAR*, THEN EVEN SURROUNDED BY FIRE...

I'LL OBSERVE FROM HERE.

IT MAY BE *CRUEL*-- BUT I, TOO, WALK THE WAY OF THE *SWORD.* I *MUST* KNOW!

33

He had once seen his father pile gravestones together to build a shelter from raging flames.

But here there were no gravestones, no stones at all. He was in the middle of parched grassland, a place of slash-and-burn fields.

There was only a small patch of muddy marsh that had greedily absorbed the rain of the previous night. There was mud enough, perhaps, to trip a child's feet. But it was hardly deep enough to burrow into until the blaze had passed.

Weeks of wet weather had kept the farmers from preparing their fields.

Now they lit their fires even though the rain had barely lifted.

Thus the flames were slow, the swamp still muddy.

Enough to prolong a boy's life.

GOOSH GOOSH

GLOP

35

If it were the grass that was burning...

...then the grass could be covered with mud to keep it from catching.

In the world of adults...

...they would have called it a firewall.

A simple, elegant answer.

But how many adults would have thought of it, face to face with the encroaching lines of death?

38

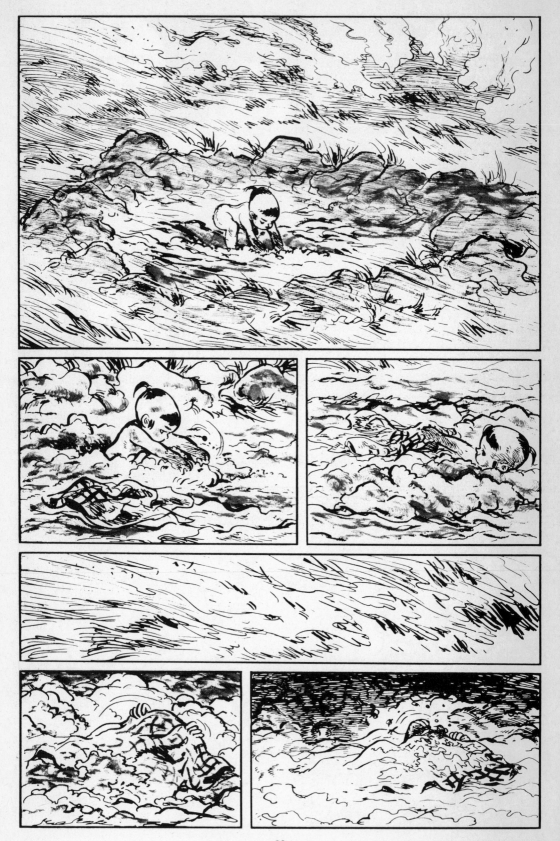

39

The sudden wind allowed no smoke to curl on the ground.

Truly he was a child born under a lucky star.

IN THE FACE OF *DISASTER* HE NEITHER *CRIED* NOR CALLED FOR *HELP.*

EVEN THOUGH A *CHILD,* HE KNEW THERE IS *LIFE* IN *DEATH,* AND HE WAS NOT AFRAID.

HE *GREETED* DEATH WITH RESIGNATION. TRULY A CHILD WITH *SHISHOGAN.*

MY EYES DID *NOT* DECEIVE ME...

NANMU. *

NANMU.--AN INVOCATION OF THE BUDDHA, SEEKING MERCY ON THE DEAD.

SLUB
SLUB

YAII!

PA...PA

IT'S A KID!

THUMP

H- HELP!

COME QUICK! IT'S A KID!

44

THIS BOY WAS CAUGHT IN A BRUSH FIRE! HE WAS *HIDING* IN THE *MUD*!

INCREDIBLE!

IN THE MUD? HE SURVIVED!?

YESSIR. HE ESCAPED THE SMOKE, CAME OUT WITHOUT A BURN.

IS HE *YOUR* BOY, SAMURAI, SIR?

PLEASE LET US THROUGH!

B- BUT...

THE POOR THING'S ON HIS LAST LEGS. HE'S *PASSED OUT*.

WE HAVE TO WASH HIM AND GET HIM TAKEN CARE OF QUICK!

I'LL BET HE WAS *SCARED*!

BUT HE'S A *LUCKY* LITTLE KID! IT'S A *MIRACLE* HE'S ALIVE!

LUCKY CHILD? YOU THINK HE WAS SAVED BY LUCK?!

W-WHAT ARE YOU DOING?

YOU DIDN'T CRY FOR HELP BECAUSE YOU KNEW YOU WERE SAFE WHERE YOU WERE.

YOU NEVER EVEN CRIED IN TERROR.

46

YAAARGH!

THERE! *SHISOGAN!* EYES THAT ONLY A *WARRIOR* STAINED WITH THE BLOOD OF COUNTLESS KILLING FIELDS CAN HAVE!

EVEN I-- I WHO HAVE RAISED MY SWORD SO OFTEN IN SLAUGHTER-- HAVE NEVER REACHED THAT LEVEL!

HOW HAS THIS MERE *BABE* ACHIEVED SUCH MASTERY?

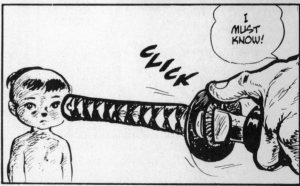

CLICK

I MUST KNOW!

AH! *SUIO ZANBATO!* THE HORSE-SLASHING STANCE OF THE *SUIO* SCHOOL!

CAN THIS *BE?!* CAN THIS *REALLY* BE?!

A child of fate, responding to the aura of death emanating from his opponent.

48

YOU'RE NO CHILD!

YOU'RE THE ONLY SHISHOGAN I'M TO MEET IN THIS LIFE!

PAPA!

WHAT!?

49

I AM *JIZAMON IKI* OF THE *TAMIYA ICHIDEN* SCHOOL.

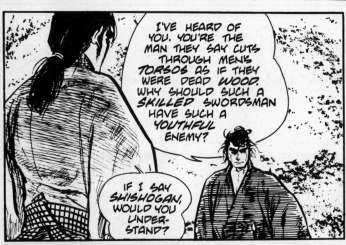

I'VE HEARD OF YOU. YOU'RE THE MAN THEY SAY CUTS THROUGH MEN'S *TORSOS* AS IF THEY WERE DEAD *WOOD*. WHY SHOULD SUCH A *SKILLED* SWORDSMAN HAVE SUCH A *YOUTHFUL* ENEMY?

IF I SAY *SHISHOGAN*, WOULD YOU UNDER- STAND?

ANY MAN WHO LIVES BY THE SWORD AND WOULD *DIE* BY THE SWORD SEEKS TO ACHIEVE *SHISHOGAN*.

I AM *ITTO OGAMI*. PREPARE FOR *SUIO-STYLE ZANBATO!*

READY!

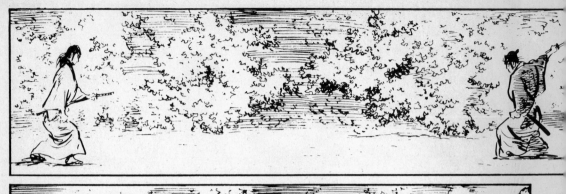

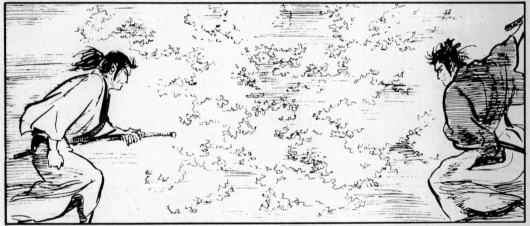

57

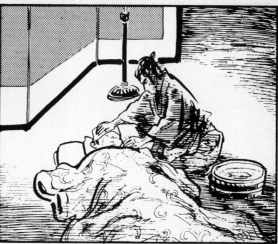

The final frost of winter lay white upon the charred fields. With the passing of this *parting frost*, the season would call forth the new, fresh green of spring.

But for this fated father and son, denied their future, when would spring ever come again...?

KAZUO KOIKE

Kazuo Koike is considered to be one of Japan's most successful writers and a master scriptwriter for the graphic story genre. He is perhaps best known in the U.S. for his screenplay for the feature film "Shogun Assassin," a re-edited version of the Japanese film "Kozure Okami," based on the **Lone Wolf and Cub** stories. Mr. Koike currently operates a publishing/production company for comics, Studio Ship, Inc., which publishes the works of Japan's major comics writers and artists in both book and magazine format. Mr. Koike is also the founder of Gekiga-Sonjuko, a school which offers a two year course for aspiring professional artists and writers.

GOSEKI KOJIMA

Goseki Kojima made his debut as a comic artist in 1967 with "Oboro-Junin-Cho." With his unique style Mr. Kojima created a new form of expressive visual interpretation for the graphic storytelling medium, and established for himself a position as a master craftsman with his ground-breaking work on **Lone Wolf and Cub**. Other works by Mr. Kojima in collaboration with Mr. Koike are "Kawaite Soro," "Kubikiri Asa," "Hanzo-No-Mon," "Tatamidori Kasajiro," "Do-Chi-Shi," and "Bohachi Bushido."

小池一夫

小島剛夕

NEXT MONTH

Both the Lone Wolf and his cub live by *Meifu Mado*: the dark road to hell. But can Itto Ogami sacrifice his own son when Daigoro becomes the pawn in the scheme of samurai bounty hunters seeking the head of the Lone Wolf?

来月